THUS SPOKE BHARTRIHARI

THUS SPOKE BHARTRIHARI

A Sanskrit Classic by Bhartrihari

A Selection from *Niti, Śringar* and *Vairagya Śatak* with their poetic English renderings

Ramesh Chandra Shah

rajpal

Price : (Rupees One Hundred Fifty) (Rs. 150.00)
Ist Edition : 2010
ISBN : 978-81-7028-805-3
THUS SPOKE BHARTRIHARI (English renderings of Sanskrit Classic *'BHARTRIHARI ŚATAK')* by Ramesh Chandra Shah

RAJPAL & SONS
Kashmere Gate, Delhi-110 006
website : www.rajpalpublishing.com
e-mail : mail@rajpalpublishing.com

For
Prof. Govind Chandra Pande
&
Mukund Lath
Whose translations from Sanskrit into Hindi
are as unique
as their original works

Contents

Preface

These translations, or rather transcreations from Bhartrihari were attempted by me about half a century ago in a mood of delighted youthful discovery. Earlier I had waded through a sea of Indological literature which the personal library of Jayanti Pant—a Shantiniketan scholar—had made accessible to me. The intense enthusiasm generated through this addiction propelled me towards the painful process of learning Sanskrit through its best literary exemplars—a task, which was made easy by her helpful guidance, who thus enabled me to appreciate the distinct superiority of a verse-rendering of the Gita by Charles Wilkins—the first European translator of that philosophical poem—to the prose rendering of the same text by others. I don't remember to have read Bhartrihari under her tutelage; her boundless and infectious enthusiasm for Kalidasa and Bhavabhuti left hardly any scope for more earth- bound and aphoristic varieties of Sanskrit poetry.

It was a chance encounter in my hometown Almora with a book on Ancient Indian Culture by Gertrude Emerson Sen that roused my curiosity about Bhartrihari. Not only what she had to say about this poet, but also the specimens she had chosen to represent him must have made an unusual impact on my sensibility; for I found myself at once immersed in the three Satakas. In fact I had a sensation akin to that of making a discovery. Here was a poet, who—

I told myself—must have known the extremes of pain and pleasure, despair and exultation, sophistry and conviction, indulgence and detachment. His poetry seemed to incorporate and justify these extremes in the most poignant manner : it compelled you to an automatic assent to the mists of legend even as your mind recoiled at the infuriating confusion that prevails in the historical-biographical accounts conjured up by traditional or modern scholarship. It was however the internal evidence of the poems themselves that seemed to reveal everything. This man must have been a king or courtier once upon a time; he must have seen through it all : the unabashed voluptuary, the remorseful moralist and the exultant ascetic—all did inhabit the self-same body and did share the same mechanism of sensibility:

You are so lucky if you can admire
The lineaments of satisfied desire
In your young bride; suck at her honey'd mouth
And let her languor in your arms retire.

The bookful blockheads preaching self-restraint
Do not consider what's really at stake.
Love's play on passionate breasts and thighs once known,
Such amorous raptures who can ever forsake.

This is from 'Śringarśatak'. But there also, he can speak in an altogether different vein. This may well sound like wishful thinking or facile attitudinizing:

The joy companionship of women brings
Ends in despair and disillusionment
Self-knowledge is the only certain good
Leading to calm of mind, all passions spent.

But, are we equally sure of our judgement, when we visit the very next stanza?

You are your own girl and your God as well
When into meditation's depths You're sucked
Love's intimacies between Man and Woman
Are no match for that self-engendered spell.

We are compelled, in spite of ourselves, to admit the presence of authentic spiritual experience behind this utterance. This is something, which could not have happened if the poet had not had a direct, unmediated experience of oneness with the Universal spirit where all dualities—even the duality of Man and Woman—dissolve and disappear. One can call it union of opposites or just Unity of Being as the poet W. B. Yeats preferred to phrase it. "Between extremities/Man runs his course"—says the poet in a poem called 'Vacillation'. Bhartrihari too can vacillate, as we have already seen, between his own models of the pleasure-principle and the reality principle. He can suddenly confront you with a terrifyingly stark choice:

There are two options; either love your woman
Enjoying all the riches of her youth;
Or, face it all alone to come to terms
With the cold comfort of Spiritual Truth.

The 'cold comfort', nevertheless, is not so cold after all. Even ascetic life is not without its rich compensations. For Bhartrihari at least, it means something much more positive than mere passive withdrawal and escape; it's a peace that borders on joy, because he has actually earned it, has strenuously 'worked' for it. The involvement, the illusion had been real enough as long as it had lasted, as the internal evidence of the verses themselves reveals to us in all their imagery and rich details. But the inevitable disgust and disillusionment with all that he has lived through has brought its own reward : liberty, which is obviously, the highest value for the poet turned sage. Vairagyasatak is Bhartrihari's own ode to this new-found 'Resolution and independence':

Blest are the saints who from all passions free
Possess their souls and live in ecstasy
With boundless space as garment and a bowl
Of rice as food and woods as company.

It's rather difficult to visualize Bhartrihari as a 'saint', because of the puritanical, body-bruising, anti-creative connotations that have unavoidably come to cling to this term. He certainly does not belong to that category of 'saints', although his poetry does confront and articulate the boredom and the horror of human life-worlds :

Drunk with delusion's ever-tempting wine
We mortals fail to see the spark Divine
Caught in the vicious whirls of nights and days
Our soul ne'er stops to think of its decline

He has known hunger, humiliation or isolation either at first hand, or through imaginative identification with all sorts of miseries of the world. There is an undercurrent of irony even in his faith; moments of anxiety and vacillation too :

My mortal moments—I know not what use
Shall they be put to; tempting is the noose
But greater far the rapture of the recluse
Or leave it all and let me serve the Muse.

He has witnessed the petty rivalries and jealousies among scholars and poets. He has known every shade of vanity and vulgarity. Even the self-knowledge he seeks and finds is not without its gloomy underside. "Why staggerest thou?'—he asks; and adds, 'These are but the world's ways'.

Bhartrihari is the authentic insider of the 'world's ways'. In fact, it is precisely the knowledge of the 'world's ways' as displayed in 'Nītiśatakam', that convinces us emotionally as well as intellectually of the sincerity of his 'Vairagyaśatakam'. His resignation rings true because his knowledge of the world rings true. He urges us to avoid 'polished men of deformed hearts'; he shows the futility of trying to please and persuade 'obstinate fools'; he tells you how 'diplomacy can disguise itself in many shapes even as a harlot does'; he has a realistic assessment of what man is capable of both ways, enabling him to distinguish between false friendship and real friendship, scholarship and pseudo-scholarship. It is this unsentimental view of human nature and human relationship that compels our assent to the values he upholds in his poetry : courage, dignity, self-reliance and freedom. But wisdom born of self-knowledge and self-control is for him the highest of all values.

Great souls while thriving keep their minds serene
Nor will they wince, when fallen on evil days.
Their wit is sharp; on scriptures they are keen
Their life unites the Hero and the Sage.

But he is painfully aware of life's little and big ironies and displays a tragicomic sense of the vagaries of Fate.

Strange doth it seem that God hath granted all
His baser kingdom food easy and pure

While reasoned man must make for things so small
Such efforts as his virtues all obscure.

... ...

How freakish are the ways of stupid Fate
Who, first a man of beauteous soul creates,
Endows him with virtues and merits great
And then, in savage fun short-lived him makes.

Even the Gods we worship are 'subdued by Fate'. But the poet goes on to proclaim that even Fate is subservient to the laws fixed by Karma.

Deeper yet we went and found,
Poor Fate itself by laws enchained
Themselves fixed by Karma,
Which alone since hath our Lord remained.

It would be unjust therefore to call Bhartrihari a fatalist. Nor would the internal evidence of the 'three centuries' permit us to categorize him as a cynical realist or even as a world-weary mystic or moralist. His poetry does lend itself to each of these partial views but actually it eludes and comprehends them all. It is the overarching wisdom of the poet that endures. That is what makes his various aphoristic appraisals of human life eloquent and enduring. It speaks to us now, in our modern condition thus :

The skies may all their secrets yield to thee
To thee may show their riches earth and sea
All this alas poor soul, availeth naught;
Know thyself and bliss perfect thine shalt be.

Each of these śatakas comprises one hundred verses (ślokas), generally condensed in four lines, sometimes two.

But as the translations of a few verses from 'Vairāgyaśatakam' by Swami Vivekanand show, it takes twice as many lines in English to express the same. The other available translations of the śatakas are by Rev. B. Hale (London, 1886), C. H. Tawney, Sri Aurobindo, Barbara Stoler Miller (1988) and Dharnidhar Sahu (2004). Sri Aurobindo translates a famous verse from Nītiśataka thus :

Some minds there are to Art and Beauty dead,
Music and Poetry on whose dull ear
Fall barren. Horns grace not their brutish head,
Tails too they lack, yet is their beasthood clear.
That Heaven ordained not upon grass their feasts
Good fortune is this for the other beasts.

I render the same verse in four lines thus :

Men with no taste for Music, Verse or Art
Like beasts in jungles play their senseless part
Save horns and tails and herbage as repast
Their lot's in every respect with them cast.

Now let us look at another verse from 'Vairagyaśataka' which Tawney translates thus :

Where many dwellers once were seen, one only now survives;
Again that home is filled with store of joyous human lives;
Then all are swept away again, thus wielding night and day
As dice, destruction's wedded powers with helpless mortals play.

This is very competently done. The stanza form chosen by Tawney is not only smooth but adequate enough to accommodate everything that the original contains. And it is not just content; form-wise too when it's compared to the original, the choice of the metrical form would seem to satisfy the most fastidious reader. But this is what I feel today. Way back in 1962, when I made the selections from Bhartrihari and rendered them into English, I had no access to these translations. The translations of Barbara Stoler Miller came only in 1990. In my blissful ignorance of all this 'before and after', I was content to work with the meager resources at my disposal. For example, although I do at times employ the much more opulent stanza form displayed above in Tawney's rendering, 1 did not think it necessary to include all the details in the original verse of Bhartrihari. I did not think my poet would be losing anything essential if I chose to translate him thus :

The house where one lived, is with many filled
Where once lived many, Death his spite has spilled
Who joined with Time, with us as pieces plays
On the vast board, the ancient game as Willed.

... ...

• The first man to read some specimens of this work was Khushwant Singh, who was then the editor of a weekly journal called 'Yojana'. Even today I can recall the strange thrill that went through me on receiving a copy of the issue that carried some of these verse—renderings under the title, 'Thus spake Bhartrihari'. Encouraged thus, I sent him some more specimens which he included in the next issue. Thereafter, I chanced upon the monthly journal called 'The Aryan Path' edited by Madame Sophia Wadia. She liked the pieces and published them serially for some issues as what she liked to call 'creative adaptations', rather than 'translations'. This naturally suited me because it appeared to flatter my vanity instead of sobering it.

Must mention here that in the earlier selection, I had not attempted any verses from 'Śringarśataka'. But,when across the yawning gulf of half a century, a friend evinced an interest in the half-forgotten, never-again-visited site and made a generous offer of reclaiming it on my behalf, it got me excited. As I nervously re-read it, I saw little reason in interfering too much with it beyond mending a couple of obvious cracks and retouching a few places. Then Vishwanathji, my friend, gently hinted that the book would be incomplete without anything from 'Śringarśataka'. 'That would make it more attractive fare for its potential readers'— he said. At first I was a little rattled by the suggestion : "How could I do at seventy what left me cold and incredulous at twenty five?" "Never mind," said he, "Now is the time to do it." I realized he was right as soon as I embarked upon this new trip. Hasn't W. B. Yeats said somewhere that 'old men must be explorers' ? And isn't Bhartrihari, in certain moods at least, our own Indian equivalent of Catullus for whom Yeats had felt such unabashed admiration?

As observed by Sri Aurobindo, "a sort of lucid density of literary structure characterized the classical Sanskrit poetry of Bhartrihari's age". While making a critical assessment of the Śatakas from this viewpoint, Sri Aurobindo further observes that these Śatakas 'underline the three leading motives of the mind of the age, its reflective interest in life and turn for high and strong thinking, its preoccupation with the enjoyment of the senses and its ascetic spiritual turn'. As Barbara Stoler Miller has put it, "Bhartrihari is expressing in his poetry a concern with salvation which is the motivating force behind Indian philosophy; there is little thought here that is not expressed earlier in the Upanishads and Bhagvada Gita. But there is uniqueness in the unorthodox juxtaposition of ideas to reinforce both the poet's own sense of suffering and his desire to escape it."

It is this 'unique, unorthodox juxtaposition of ideas' that attracts the modem reader to a poet like Bhartrihari. This unique characteristic, alongwith the subtle use of irony and paradox constitutes the charm as well as the challenge that Bhartrihari's verses offer to a translator. A translator makes himself vulnerable either way: whether s/he remains literally faithful or opts for the more imaginative way out, he or she is going to remain suspect. One nevertheless keeps hoping against hope; and I can do no better than hope that this fruit of my 'innocence'—my 'love's labour'—may not have been altogather in vain. Here I cannot help invoking Kalidasa in 'Kumārsambhava':

'Kleshah phalen punarnavatām vidhatté'

Ramesh Chandra Shah

November, 2009
M-4 Nirala Nagar, Bhadbhada Road,
Bhopal-462003

NITI ŚATAKA
नीति शतक

यां चिन्तयामि सततं मयि सा विरक्ता
साप्यन्यमिच्छति जनं स जनोऽन्यसक्तः।
अस्मत्कृते च परितुष्यति काचिदन्या
धिक् तां च तं च मदनं च इमां च मां च ॥1॥

प्रसह्य मणिम् उद्धरेत् मकरवक्त्रदंष्ट्रान्तरात्
समुद्रमपि सन्तरेत् प्रचलत् ऊर्मिमाला आकुलम्।
भुजङ्गमपि कोपितं शिरसि पुष्पवद् धारयेत्
न तु प्रतिनिविष्टमूर्खजनचित्तमधारयेत् ॥2॥

व्यालं बालमृणालतन्तुभिः असौ रोद्धुं समुज्जृम्भते
छेत्तुं वज्रमणिं शिरीषकुसुमप्रान्तेन सन्नह्यति।
माधुर्यं मधुबिन्दुना रचयितुं क्षाराम्बुधेरीहते
नेतुं वाञ्छति यः खलान् पथि सतां सूक्तैः सुधास्यन्दिभिः ॥3॥

The lady whom I always contemplate
Has given her secret love to another man;
And lo! he on another lass does wait.
Curse be on cupid, myself, her, the man.

From crocodiles we can a jewel redeem
And cross a sea by waves tumultous swept
To wear a snake on head a play might seem
But who with conceit has his patience kept?

Good men! When full of zeal you endeavour
To change the nature of an evil being
You try to chain wild beasts by stems of flower
And sugar sea for water-sweetening.

स्वायत्तम् एकान्तगुणं विधात्रा विनिर्मितं छादनमज्ञतायाः ।
विशेषतः सर्वविदां समाजे विभूषणं मौनम् पण्डितानाम् ॥4॥

यदा किंचिज्ज्ञोऽहं द्विप इव मदान्धः समभवं
तदा सर्वज्ञोऽस्मीत्यभवदवलिप्तं मम मनः ।
यदा किंचित्किंचिद् बुधजनसकाशात् अवगतम्
तदा मूर्खोऽस्मीति ज्वर इव मदो मे व्यपगतः ॥5॥

कृमिकुलचितं लालाक्लिन्नं विगन्धि जुगुप्सितं
निरुपमरसं प्रीत्या खादन्नरास्थि निरामिषम् ।
सुरपतिमपि श्वा पार्श्वस्थं विलोक्य न शङ्कते
न हि गणयति क्षुद्रो जन्तुः परिग्रहफल्गुताम् ॥6॥

हर्तुर्याति न गोचरं किमपि शं पुष्णाति यत्सर्वदा
ह्यर्थिभ्यः प्रतिपाद्यमानम् अनिशं प्राप्नोति वृद्धिं पराम् ।
कल्पान्तेष्वपि न प्रयाति निधनं विद्याख्यम् अन्तर्धनम्
येषां तान्प्रति मानमुज्झत नृपाः! कस्तैः सह स्पर्धते ॥7॥

How sound a trick is taciturnity
For dabblers in the midst of scholars deep!
The surface, smiling thus fore'er will keep
Serene and pure...a shallow mystery.

With my head fill'd with sraps of knowledge odd
Pride-swollen thought myself I omniscient.
But when amid the learned first I trod
I knew my folly; down the fever want.

Behold! the dog licking his favourite bone
Rotten and full of pus and nasty worms.
How enraptured is he: so, we must own
That what we cling to most are worthless forms.

Let scholars be reverenced by you 0 kings:
For they have treasures great that none can steal
That wealth of learning which good only brings
They scatter it and the richer for it feel.

केयूराणि न भूषयन्ति पुरुषं हारा न चन्द्रोज्ज्वला
न स्नानं न विलेपनं न कुसुमं नालङ्कृता मूर्धजाः।
वाण्येका समलङ्करोति पुरुषं या संस्कृता धार्यते
क्षीयन्ते खलु भूषणानि सततं वाग्भूषणं भूषणम् ॥8॥

विद्या नाम नरस्य रूपमधिकं प्रच्छन्नगुप्तं धनं
विद्या भोगकरी यशःसुखकरी विद्या गुरुणां गुरुः।
विद्या बन्धुजनो विदेशगमने विद्या परा देवता
विद्या राजसु पूज्यते न तु धनं विद्याविहीनः पशुः ॥9॥

प्रदानं प्रच्छन्नं गृहमुपगते सम्भ्रमविधिः
प्रियं कृत्वा मौनं सदसि कथनं चाप्युपकृतेः।
अनुत्सेको लक्ष्म्यां निरभिभवसाराः परकथाः
सतां केनोद्दिष्टं विषममसिधारा व्रतमिदम् ॥10॥

रे रे चातक! सावधानमनसा मित्र! क्षणं श्रूयता
मम्भोदा बह्वो व सन्ति गगने सर्वेऽपि नैतादृशाः
केचिद् वृष्टिभिरार्द्रयन्ति वसुधां गर्जन्ति केचिद् वृथा
यं यं पश्यसि तस्य तस्य पुरतो मा ब्रूहि दीनं वचः ॥11॥

No jewel of sparkling glory would adorn
A man unless richly endowed he be
With cultured speech of any roughness shorn
For here's a jewel from all corruptions free.

If you are man of letters, you are rich
And handsome too; Whatever you desire
Is thus within your reach—fame, wealth and friend
You are supreme, the god that all admire.

How full of thorns the path is of those men
Who strive to be good in this world of vice !
Selfless and modest, they just care for others
And guard their honour at whatever price.

O Chatak, Friend!...listen to me awhile
Why should you cringe thus?...it's a sight most shocking
The sky is strewn, no doubt, with myriad clouds
But most of them are empty, vain and mocking.

दुर्जनः परिहर्तव्योविद्ययाऽलंकृतोऽपि सन्।
मणिना भूषितः सर्पः किमसौ न भयङ्करः ॥12॥

साहित्यसंगीतकलाविहीनः साक्षात्पशुः पुच्छविषाणहीनः।
तृणन्नखादन्नपि जीवमानः तद् भागधेयं परमं पशूनाम् ॥13॥

लभेत सिकतासु तैलमपि यत्नतः पीडयन्
पिबेच्च मृगतृष्णिकासु सलिलं पिपासार्दितः।
कदाचिदपि पर्यटन् शशविषाणम् अपि आसदयेत्
न तु प्रतिनिविष्ट मूर्खजनचित्तम् आराधयेत् ॥14॥

भवन्ति नम्राः तरवः फलोद्गमैः नवाम्बुभिः दूरविलम्बिनः घनाः।
अनुद्धताः सत्पुरुषाः समृद्धिभिः स्वभाव एवैष परोपकारिणाम् ॥15॥

Avoid the polished man of heart deformed
Immersed though he in depths of learning be.
We meet some snakes with jewel-embellished head
Does it then mean—they are from poison free?

Men with no taste for music, verse or art
Like beasts in jungles play their senseless part.
Save horn and tail and herbage as repast
Their lot's in every respect with them cast.

Our toil may extract oil even from sand;
And thirsty men in desert find a lake;
Horned hare even we may see on some land;
Fools obstinate we ne'er can happy make.

Laden with fruit the trees bend themselves down;
And clouds in water rich soar never high.
In great men, modesty can live with crown
Men of real greatness are of glory shy.

खल्वाटो दिवसेश्वरस्य किरणैः सन्तापितो मस्तके
वाञ्छन्देशमनातपं विधिवशात्तालस्य मूलं गतः।
तत्राप्यस्य महाफलेन पतता भग्नं सशब्दं शिरः
प्रायो गच्छति यत्र भाग्यरहितस्तत्रैव यान्त्यापदः ॥16॥

शशिदिवाकरयोः ग्रहपीड़नं गजभुजङ्गमयोरपि बन्धनम्।
मतिमताञ्चविलोक्य दरिद्रतां विधिरहो बलवानिति मे मतिः ॥17॥

विपदि धैर्यमथाभ्युदये क्षमा
सदसि वाक्पटुता युधि विक्रमः।
यशसि चाभिरुचिर्व्यसनं श्रुतौ
प्रकृतिसिद्धमिदं हि महात्मनाम् ॥18॥

Sore oppressed by the burning heat of day,
A baldicoot, his head as if on flame
Perceived a shady palm beside the way
And blessing his good luck under it came.

No sooner had he at his ease reclined
Than fell a massive nut breaking his head.
Forsooth wherever goes the ill-destined
Misfortunes on his heels will always tread.

To eclipse must the sun and moon succumb;
The elephant must find itself in ropes;
The scholar must forever face starvation;
Fate is alas, far stronger than our hopes.

Great souls, while thriving, keep their mind serene,
Nor will they wince, when fall'n on evil days.
Their wit is sharp, on scriptures they are keen.
Their life unites the Hero and the sage.

हिंसाशून्यमयत्नलभ्यमशनं धात्रा मरुत्कल्पितं
व्यालानां पशवस्तृणाङ्कुरभुजः सृष्टाः स्थलीशायिनः।
संसारार्णवलङ्घनक्षमधियां वृत्तिः कृता सा नृणां
यामन्वेषयता प्रयान्ति सततं सर्वे समाप्तिं गुणाः ॥19॥

क्षुत्क्षामोऽपि जराकृशोऽपि शिथिलप्राणोऽपि कष्टां दशा-
मापन्नोऽपि विपन्नदीधितिरपि प्राणेषु नश्यत्स्वपि।
मत्तेभेन्द्रविभिन्न कुम्भ पिशितग्रासैकबद्धस्पृहः
किं जीर्णं तृणमत्ति मानमहतामग्रेसरः केसरी ॥20॥

प्रायः कन्दुकपातेनोत्पतत्यार्यः पतन्नपि
तथा त्वनार्यः पतति मृत्पिण्डपतनं यथा ॥21॥

छिन्नोऽपि रोहति तरुः क्षीणोऽप्युपचीयते पुनश्चन्द्रः।
इति विमृशन्तः सन्तः संतप्यन्ते न विप्लुता लोके ॥22॥

Strange doth it seem that God hath granted all
His baser kingdom food easy and pure;
While reason'd man must make for things so small
Such efforts as his virtues all obscure.

Age may the lion of his strength deprive;
Rob him of his self-respect it can not.
However oppressed by hunger, he will strive
And wait till he himself his prey has caught.

Men of character even when they fall
Do rise to greater heights than heretofore
Their course resembling an elastic ball;
The rest—like muddy things, can rise no more.

"Cut thou a tree : t'will spring to life again.
And, soon the crescent moon regains her might".
The wisest reason thus; and shadows vain
of worldly sufferings cannot them affright.

निन्दन्तु नीतिनिपुणाः यदि वा स्तुवन्तु
लक्ष्मीः समाविशतु गच्छतु वा यथेष्टम्।
अद्यैव वा मरणमस्तु युगान्तरे वा
न्याय्यात्पथः प्रविचलन्ति पदं न धीराः ॥23॥

यस्यास्ति वित्तं स नरः कुलीनः
स पण्डितः स श्रुतवान्गुणज्ञः
स एव वक्ता स च दर्शनीयः
सर्वे गुणाः काञ्चनमाश्रयन्ति ॥24॥

कुसुमस्तबकस्येव द्वयी वृत्तिर्मनस्विनः।
मूर्ध्नि वा सर्वलोकस्य विशीर्येत वनेऽथवा ॥25॥

कर्मायत्तं फलं पुंसां बुद्धिः कर्मानुसारिणी।
तथापि सुधिया भाव्यं सुविचार्यैव कुर्वता ॥26॥

High souls adopt a path and stick to it
To idle sneers of the world immune.
For praise or censure care they not a whit,
No frowns of fate would make their purpose swoon.

He who has wealth, his shall it be to win
The glamours of high birth and learning's weight.
All sorts of virtues strive to dwell within
The man of gold and not of spirit great.

High-minded men of nature truly proud
Are like a bunch of blossoms in full bloom.
That either will adorn the brow divine
or in the lone wood meet its mournful doom.

Though deeds of previous births determine fruits
of present ones and shape our thinking too;
Yet ignorant of future we must strive
To put our best into everything we do.

सृजति तावदशेषगुणाकरं पुरुषरत्नमलङ्करणं भुवः।
तदपि तत्क्षणभङ्गि करोति चेदहह कष्टमपण्डितता विधेः ॥27॥

मनसि वचसि काये पुण्यपीयूषपूर्णा-
स्त्रिभुवनमुपकारश्रेणिभिः प्रीणयन्तः।
परगुणपरमाणून् पर्वतीकृत्य नित्यं
निजहृदि विकसन्तः सन्ति सन्तः कियन्तः ॥28॥

रत्नैर्महाब्धेस्तुतुषुर्न देवाः न भेजिरे भीमविषेण भीतिम्।
सुधां विना न प्रययुर्विरामं न निश्चितार्थाद्विरमन्ति धीराः ॥29॥

लाङ्गूलचालनमधश्चरणावपातं
भूमौ निपत्य वदनोदरदर्शनं च।
श्वा पिण्डदस्य कुरुते गजपुङ्गवस्तु
धीरं विलोकयति चाटुशतैश्च भुङ्क्ते ॥30॥

How freakish are the ways of stupid Fate,
Who first a man of beauteous soul creates;
Endows him with virtues and merits great;
And then in savage fun short-lived him makes.

True generous souls, whose goodness knows no bound
Whom you find always prone to magnify
Merits of others; though of judgement sound
They treat the whole world as their family.

Did sea-born treasures make th' immortals cease
From their set goal?...Could poison fatal chill
Their hearts aspiring for celestial mead?
Stop not till you achieve the goal you will.

This dog can wag its tail to any man
Who may the crumbs remaining cast his way.
Contrast this slave with noble elephant
Who is entreated long that eat he may.

सत्याऽनृता च परुषा प्रियवादिनी च
हिंस्रा दयालुरपि चार्थपरा वदान्या।
नित्यव्यया प्रचुरनित्यधनागमा च
वाराङ्गनेव नृपनीतिरनेकरूपा ॥31॥

यद्धात्रा निजभालपट्टलिखितं स्तोकं महद्वा धनं
तत्प्राप्नोति मरुस्थलेऽपि नितरां मेरौ ततो नाधिकम्।
तद्धीरो भव वित्तवत्सु कृपणां वृत्तिं वृथा मा कृथाः।
कूपे पश्य पयोनिधावपि घटो गृह्णाति तुल्यं जलम् ॥32॥

जाड्यं ह्रीमति गण्यते व्रतरुचौ दम्भः शुचौ कैतवं
शूरे निर्घृणता मुनौ विमतिता दैन्यं प्रियालापिनि।
तेजस्विन्यवलिप्तता मुखरता वक्तर्यशक्तिः स्थिरे
तत्को नाम गुणो भवेत् स गुणिनां यो दुर्जनैर्नाङ्कितः ॥33॥

आरम्भगुर्वी क्षयिणी क्रमेण लघ्वी पुरा वृद्धिमती च पश्चात्।
दिनस्यपूर्वार्द्ध परार्द्धभिन्ना छायेव मैत्री खलसज्जनानाम् ॥34॥

How diplomacy can itself disguise
In many shapes e'en as a harlot does.
It can be true or false, foolish or wise.
Selfish or generous, sweet or venomous.

Shaped once, the pitcher dipped in well or sea
Takes equal fluid. Rest content with thy lot.
Fret as thou mayest, what hath been granted thee
For all thy stuggles, shall not grow a jot.

Virtue itself 'scapes not tongues malignant:
The saintly man is called a Hypocrite;
Servile and coward—gentle and polite;
Heartless—the strong-will'd; Dunce—the reticent.

False friendship like the shadows of forenoon
Goes on decreasing; and at last dies out,
While friendship true like that of afternoon
Though scant at first achieves full stature soon.

सम्पत्सु महतां वित्तं भवेदुत्पलकोमलम्।
आपत्सु च महाशैलशिला सङ्घातकर्कशम् ॥35॥

सन्तप्तायसि संस्थितस्य पयसो नामापि न ज्ञायते
मुक्ताकारतया तदेव नलिनीपत्रस्थितं राजते
स्वात्यां सागरशुक्तिमध्यपतितं तन्मौक्तिकं जायते
प्रायेणाधममध्यमोत्तमजुषामेवं विधा वृत्तयः ॥36॥

पापान्निवारयति योजयते हिताय
गुह्यं निगूहति गुणान्प्रकटीकरोति।
आपद्गतञ्च न जहाति ददाति काले
सन्मित्रलक्षणमिदं प्रवदन्ति सन्तः ॥37॥

पद्माकरं दिनकरो विकचीकरोति
चन्द्रो विकासयति कैरवचक्रवालम्।
नाभ्यर्थितो जलधरोऽपि जलं ददाति
सन्तः स्वयं परहितेषु कृताभियोगाः ॥38॥

The hearts of great men in affluent days
Are flower-like,...selfless and sweet and kind.
When mock'd with Misery's darkest known visage
Firm like the mountain-rocks them you will find.

A water-drop on red-hot iron hurl;
It disappears; the same now settled on
The flower-petal glitters like a pearl.
It's out of contact, good and bad have grown.

Know him alone to be a friend indeed
Who warns and saves against and from pitfalls;
Who clings to you in distress; helps in need
And hiding faults, to all your worth extols.

The Bounteous Sun sustains the Kamal's life
The Kumudas are nourished by the moon;
Unasked the clouds refresh the earth with rain
Great souls their life to selfless acts attune.

क्षान्तिश्चेत्कवचेन किं किमरिभिः क्रोधोऽस्ति चेद्देहिनां
ज्ञातिश्चेदनलेन किं यदि सुहृद्दिव्यौषधैः किं फलम्।
किं सर्पैर्यदि दुर्जनाः किमु धनैर्विद्याऽनवद्या यदि
व्रीडा चेत्किमु भूषणैः सुकविता यद्यस्ति राज्येन किम् ॥39॥

वरं पर्वतदुर्गेषु, भ्रान्तं वनचरैः सह।
न मूर्खजनसम्पर्कः सुरेन्द्रभुवनेष्वपि ॥40॥

प्रारभ्यते न खलु विघ्नभयेन नीचैः
प्रारभ्य विघ्नविहता विरमन्ति मध्याः।
विघ्नैः पुनः पुनरपि प्रतिहन्यमानाः
प्रारब्धमुत्तमजनाः न परित्यजन्ति ॥41॥

तानीन्द्रियाण्यविकलानि तदेव नाम
सा बुद्धिरप्रतिहता वचनं तदेव।
अर्थोष्मणा विरहितः पुरुषः स एव
त्वन्यः क्षणेन भवतीति विचित्रमेतत् ॥42॥

If thou hast forgiveness sweet,
What use for armour shall thou find?
What deadlier foe's there if,
Retainest thou anger in mind?
No viper is more venomous
Than the malignant villain
What medicine dost thou seek
If one good friend thou hast again?

Better wander in the hills
And jungles with the beasts
Than in the society of fools
In heaven enjoy feasts.

The vulgar would never begin
For fear of much impediment.
The average does begin, but his
Courage attacked by odds is spent.
Whatever be the hindrances
Undaunted by their frequency
The noble with a task in hand
Pursues it with persistency.

The senses are the same and so the name.
And speech and wit are trenchant as before.
But since the warmth of wealth he hath no more,
He's changed and crumbled to the dust his fame.

जाड्यं धियो हरति सिंचति वाचि सत्यं
मानोन्नतिं दिशति पापमपाकरोति।
चेतः प्रसादयति दिक्षु तनोति कीर्तिं
सत्संगतिः कथय किं न करोति पुंसाम् ॥43॥

एते सत्पुरुषाः परार्थघटकाः स्वार्थान्परित्यज्य ये
सामान्यास्तु परार्थमुद्यमभृतः स्वार्थाविरोधेन ये
तेऽमी मानुषराक्षसाः परिहतं स्वार्थाय निघ्नंति ये
ये निघ्नन्ति निरर्थकं परहितं ते के न जानीमहे ॥44॥

क्षीरेणात्मगतोदकाय हि गुणाः दत्ताः पुरा तेऽखिलाः
क्षीरोत्तापमवेक्ष्य तेन पयसा ह्यात्मा कृशानौ हुतः
गन्तुं पावकमुन्मनस्तदभवद् दृष्ट्वा तु मित्रापदं
युक्तं तेन जलेन शाम्यति सतां मैत्री पुनस्त्वीदृशी ॥45॥

पत्रं नैव करीरविटपे यदि दोषो वसन्तस्य किं
नोलूकोऽप्यवलोकते यदि दिवा सूर्यस्य किं दूषणम्।
धारा नैव पतन्ति चातकमुखे मेघस्य किं दूषणं
यत्पूर्वं विधिना ललाटलिखितं तन्मार्जितुं कः क्षमः ॥46॥

Good friendship can our wit and sense quicken
Inculcate truth and point the path of fame
It makes us happy, helps to spread good name
What wonders can society work in men.

Selfless souls who live for others are of this wide earth the cream,
Those regarding self, still doing good to others next thou deem,
Monsters they, who ruin their fellow out of motive self centred;
What shall we but call the motiveless villain of crimes abhorred!

Look : the milk has given to water all its qualities at once
And the water burned itself to save the milk from heat intense.
Distress't by his friend's agony, mounts the milk to follow him
Soften'd then alone with water; can such love grow ever dim?

If karil tree have no leaf on't, is the Spring to blame here?
And if owls be blind in daytime, is the sun at fault there?
Thirsty if the rains leave Chatak, shall we call unjust the cloud?
Can what Fate has foreordained be by frail mortals blotted out?

नमस्यामो देवान्ननु हतविधेस्तेऽपि वशगा
विधिर्वन्द्यः सोऽपि प्रतिनियतकर्मैकफलदः।
फलं कर्मायत्तं यदि किममरैः किंच विधिना
नमस्तत्कर्मभ्यो विधिरपि न येभ्यः प्रभवति ॥47॥

को लाभो गुणिसंगमः किमसुखं प्राज्ञेतरैः संगतिः
का हानिः समयच्युतिर्निपुणता का धर्मतत्त्वे रतिः
कः शूरो विजितेन्द्रियः प्रियतमा काऽनुव्रता किं धनं
विद्या किं सुखमप्रवासगमनं राज्यं किमाज्ञाफलम् ॥48॥

वाञ्छा सज्जनसंगमे परगुणे प्रीतिर्गुरौ नम्रता
विद्यायां व्यसनं स्वयोषिति रतिः लोकापवादाद् भयम्।
भक्तिः शूलिनि शक्तिरात्मदमने संसर्गमुक्तिः खले
येष्वेते निवसन्ति निर्मलगुणास्तेभ्यो नरेभ्यो नमः ॥49॥

Bow we though before the Gods, yet they too are subdued
by Fate.
Reasoning thus, we Fate alone as our object of worship
viewed.
Deeper yet we went and found poor Fate itself by laws
enchained
Themselves fixed by Karma, which alone since hath our
lord remained.

What the greatest gain in earth and what the awful
chagrin most
But the friendship of the wisest and the Blockhead's
empty boast
Waste of time—the dearest loss; best gift—command of
secret lore
Bravest, who subdues his self; and richest—man of
learning pure.

Love of good and wise society, reverence for the elder
ones;
Thirst for knowledge, and a heart untouched with winds
of temptations;
Fear of God, restraint of self, detachment from the
world of vice;
Homage be mine to a man in whom reside these virtues
nice.

ŚRINGAR ŚATAKA

शृंगार शतक

अदर्शने दर्शनमात्रकामा दृष्ट्वा परिष्वंगरसैकलोलाः।
आलिंगितायां पुनरायताक्ष्यामाशास्महे विग्रहयोरभेदम् ॥1॥

मधुरयं मधुरैरपि कोकिला कलकलैर्मलयस्य च वायुभिः
विरहिणः प्रणिहन्ति शरीरिणो विपदि हन्त सुधापि विषायते ॥2॥

पान्थस्त्रीविरहानलाहुतिकथामातन्वतीमञ्जरी
माकन्देषु पिकाङ्गनाभिरधुना सोत्कण्ठमालोक्यते।
अप्येते नवपाटलपरिमलप्राग्भारपाटञ्चरा
वान्ति क्लान्तिवितानतानवकृतः श्रीखण्डशैलानिलाः ॥3॥

How amorous instincts have us in full thrall!
While absence makes me pine her to behold,
Beholding breeds a wish to draw her nigh,
And then I long her thus forever to hold.

In sweetest season when the cuckoo's song
Floats in the air with fragrance laden sweet
Of flowers, the love-lorn soul repines among
Fond memories of his Love in lone retreat.

What joy is cuckoo's—leaning fondly on
The Mango twig with flowers studded sweet!
But these soft strains fall heavily upon
That lady...pining in her lone retreat.

वियदुपचितमेघं भूमयः कन्दलिन्यो
नवकुटजकदम्बामोदिनी गन्धवाहाः
शिखिकुलकलकेकारावरम्या वनान्ताः
सुखिनमसुखिनं वा सर्वमुत्कण्ठयन्ति ॥4॥

असाराः सन्त्वेते विरतिविरसायासविषया
जुगुप्सन्तां यद्वा ननु सकलदोषास्पदमिति।
तथाप्यन्तस्तत्त्वे प्रणिहितधियामप्यतिबल-
स्तदीयोऽनाख्येयः स्फुरति हृदये कोऽपि महिमा ॥5॥

किमिह बहुभिरुक्तैर्युक्तिशून्यैः प्रलापै--
र्द्वयमपि पुरुषाणां सर्वदा सेवनीयम्
अभिनवमदलीलालालसं सुन्दरीणां
स्तनभरपरिखिन्नं यौवनं वा वनं वा ॥6॥

शंभुस्वयंभुहरयो हरिणेक्षणानां
येनाक्रियत सततं गृहकर्मदासाः।
वाचामगोचरचरित्रविचित्रताय,
तस्मै नमो भगवते कुसुमायुधाय ॥7॥

The sky o'ercast with clouds of darkest hue,
Sprouts dancing on the bosom of the earth;
Cool air, the peacock bounding, blossoms new,
Give rise to yearnings of amorous birth.

Pursuit of pleasures only ends in pain,
Still do our bodies pamper we with zest.
They curse the flesh all day, but then again
Voluptuous passions sway their feeble breast.

Enough of empty logic; I have found
Two goods in life;—either in amorous moods
With carnal pleasures let thy bed abound
Or seek the Peace of jungle solitudes.

Enthralled by doe-eyed wives, even Godlike Brahma
Vishnu and Shiva submit to your sway
O'er them O Camdeo, mighty lord of Love!
No better than domestic servants—they

भ्रूचातुर्याकुंचिताक्षाः कटाक्षाः स्निग्धा वाचो लज्जितांताश्च हासाः ।
लीलामन्दं प्रस्थितं सस्मितं च स्त्रीणामेतद्भूषणं चायुधं च ॥8॥

वक्त्रं चन्द्रविडम्बि पङ्कजपरीहासक्षमे लोचने
वर्णः स्वर्णमपाकरिष्णुरलिनीजिष्णुः कचानां चयः ।
वक्षोजाविभकुम्भविभ्रमहरौगुर्वी नितम्बस्थली
वाचोहारि च मार्दवं युवतिषु स्वाभाविकं मण्डनम् ॥9॥

द्रष्टव्येषु किमुत्तमं मृगदृशां प्रेमप्रसन्नं मुखं
घ्रातव्येष्वपि किं तदास्यपवनः श्राव्येषु किं तद्वचः ।
किं स्वाद्येषु तदोष्ठपल्लवरसः स्पर्शेषु किं तत्तनु-
र्ध्येयं किं नवयौवनं सहृदयैः सर्वत्र तद्विभ्रमः ॥10॥

नूनं हि ते कविवरा विपरीतबोधा
ये नित्यमाहुरबला इति कामिनीनाम् ।
याभिर्विलोलतरतारकदृष्टिपातैः
शक्रादयोऽपि विजिता अबलाः कथं ताः ॥11॥

What ornaments-cum-lethal weapons are
Employed by women to annihilate
Defenceless men—slant glances, cryptic smiles,
Delicious accents and bewitching gait!

What other embellishments these damsels need
With moon-like faces and those lotus eyes!
Endowed by Nature as they are indeed
Honeybee hair and elephantine thighs!

What's the best visual? Love's ecstatic glance.
And the best fragrance? That which doth enhance
The thrill of getting drunk with her deep kisses.
Most worth remembering? Each and every stance.

Poets who say—women are weaker sex
Are either fools; or wilfully obtuse.
The wiles that even in trance a yogi vex
No masculine strength can resist or refuse.

केशाः संयमिनः श्रुतेरपि परं पारं गते लोचने
चान्तर्वक्त्रमपि स्वभावशुचिभिः कीर्णं द्विजानां गणैः।
मुक्तानां सतताधिवासरुचिरं वक्षोजकुम्भद्वयं
चेत्थं तन्वि वपुः प्रशान्तमपि ते क्षोभं करोत्येव नः ॥12॥

तस्याः स्तनौ यदि घनौ जघनं विहारि
वक्त्रं च चारु तव चित्त किमाकुलत्वम्।
पुण्यं कुरुष्व यदि तेषु तवास्ति वाञ्छा
पुण्यैर्विना नहि भवन्ति समीहितार्थाः ॥13॥

उरसि निपतितानां स्रस्तधम्मिल्लकानां
मुकुलितनयनानां किंचिदुन्मीलितानाम्।
सुरतजनितखेदस्विन्नगण्डस्थलाना-
मधुरमधु वधूनां भाग्यवन्तः पिबन्ति ॥14॥

रागस्यागारमेकं नरकशतमहादुःख संप्राप्ति हेतुः
मोहस्य उत्पत्तिबीजं जलधरपटलं ज्ञानताराधिपस्य।
कन्दर्पस्यैकमित्रं प्रकटितविविध स्पष्टदोषप्रबन्धं
लोकेऽस्मिन्न ह्यनर्थव्रजकुसुभवनं यौवनादन्यदस्ति ॥15॥

Look at hairstyle!—Isn't that a model of great self-
restraint?
Eyes that stretch beyond the ears bespeak a wisdom
beyond saint,
Necklace of pearls on the breasts—aren't they the pearls
of perfect bliss?
Why should then cause unrest to me this live embodiment
of Peace?

If you seek blessings from those breasts and thighs
And on that heavenly face to feed your eyes,
Good deeds alone can such rare harvest reap
Above the average you will have to rise.

You are so lucky if you can admire
The lineaments of satisfied desire
In your young bride, suck at her honey'd mouth
And let her languor in your arms retire.

Let me recount the ills of youth accursed :
Home of attachment; of all hells the worst.
As known accomplice of the God of Love
Youth clouds the moon of wisdom, traps in lust.

संसारेऽस्मिन्नसारे परिणतितरले द्वे गती पण्डितानां
तत्त्वज्ञानामृताम्भ-प्लवलुलितधियां यातु कालः कदाचित्।
नो चेन्मुग्धाङ्गनानां स्तनजघनघनाभोगसंसर्गिणीनां
स्थूलोपस्थस्थलीषु स्थगितकरतलस्पर्शलोलोद्यमानाम् ॥16॥

स्मृता भवति पापाय दृष्ट्वा चोन्मादकारिणी
स्पृष्टा भवति मोहाय सा नाम दयिता कथम् ॥17॥

तावदेवामृतमयी यावल्लोचनगोचरा।
चक्षुःपथादतीता तु विषादप्यतिरिच्यते ॥18॥

नामृतं न विषं किंचिदेकां मुक्त्वा नितम्बिनीम्।
सैवामृतलता रक्ता विरक्ता विषवल्लरी ॥19॥

In this world of transient shadows, is there any certain good?
Yes, there are two precious objects worth-engaging your manhood.
Final facts are there to pursue for the metaphysical mind;
Meanwhile in my beloved's body I can my salvation find.

Remembering her alone is cause enough
Of disturbance; but seeing her makes you mad.
Her slightest contact turns you into a fool
And still you call her beloved—oh, how sad!

So long as she is still within your gaze
You feel you're being fed on honey-dew.
But, out of sight, she leaves you in a daze
As if a poisoned arrow has hit you.

There is no poison, no ambrosial water—
Except your woman—Listen what I tell.
So long as she loves you, you are in Heaven
But, once estranged, you find yourself in hell.

आवर्तः संशयानामविनयभवनं पत्तनं साहसानां
दोषाणां संनिधानं कपटशतमयं क्षेत्रमप्रत्ययानाम्।
स्वर्गद्वारस्य विघ्नो नरकपुरमुखं सर्वमायाकरण्डं
स्त्रीयन्त्रं केन सृष्टं विषममृतमयं प्राणिनामेकपाशः ॥20॥

जल्पन्ति सार्धमन्येन पश्यन्त्यन्यं सविभ्रमाः।
हृदये चिन्तयन्त्यन्यं प्रियः को नाम योषिताम् ॥21॥

कामिनीकायकान्तारे कुचपर्वतदुर्गमे
मा संचर मनः पान्थ तत्रास्ते स्मरतस्करः ॥22॥

इह हि मधुरगीतं नृत्यमेतद्रसोऽयं
स्फुरति परिमलोऽसौ स्पर्श एषस्तनानाम्।
इति हतपरमार्थैरिन्द्रियैर्भ्राम्यमाणः
स्वहितकरणदक्षैः पञ्चभिर्वञ्चितोऽस्मि ॥23॥

Whose instrument is woman?—none can tell
Eternal bondage, bliss-cum-curse of creatures
Whirlpool of doubts and city of adventures
Impediment to Heaven, gateway to Hell.

Her mind is engaged somewhere else,
While she gives you her word.
And, all this while her eyes have been
Entangled with a third.

Most dangerous terrain this—a woman's body!
A robber called the God of Love lives there.
Don't let these hills and dales detain you long
You've more to lose than they've to offer here.

Her speech is music and her movements dance,
Her breasts, her sense of touch; her breath fragrance,
Thus all five senses, so mortgaged to pleasure
Of winning back my freedom, there's no chance.

वेश्यासौ मदनज्वाला रूपेन्धनसमेधिता।
कामिभिर्यत्र हूयन्ते यौवनानि धनानि च ॥24॥

विरहोऽपि संगमः खलु परस्परं संगतं मनोयेषाम्।
यद्हृदयविघटितः संगमोऽपि विरहं विशेषयति ॥25॥

सदा योगाभ्यासव्यसनवशयोः आत्ममनसः
रविच्छिन्ना मैत्री स्फुरति कृतिनस्तस्य किमु तैः।
प्रियाणाम् आलापैः अधरमधुभिः वक्त्रविधुभिः
सनिःश्वासामोदैः सकुचकलशाश्लेषसुरतैः ॥26॥

यदासीदज्ञानं स्मरतिमिर संचारजनितं
तदा दृष्टं नारीमयमिदमशेषं जगदपि
इदानीमस्माकं पटुतरविवेकाञ्जनजुषां
समीभूता दृष्टिस्त्रिभुवनमपि ब्रह्म मनुते ॥27॥

Harlots work overtime and fuel themselves
To feed this ancient altar of desire
Where people blinded by their passion flock
To offer youth and wealth to Primal Fire.

Minds attuned to each other
Are close though far-removed
But as for minds estranged,
I have never approved
Their living under the same roof.
They hardly hear each other
A sea rolls between them
There's neither rhyme nor rhythm.

You are your own girl and your God as well
When into meditation's depths you're sucked.
Love's intimacies between Man and Woman,
Are no match for that self-engendered spell.

Ignorance caused by Eros–God of Love
Had marred my vision, womanizing it.
Self-knowledge unsexed me, restored my wholeness.
Now, I see SELF everywhere from this summit.

तावदेव कृतिनां हृदि स्फुरत्येष निर्मलविवेकदीपकः।
यावदेव न कुरङ्गचक्षुषां ताड्यते चपललोचनाञ्चलैः ॥28॥

भवति वचसि सङ्गत्यागमुद्दिश्य वार्ता
श्रुतमुखरमुखानां केवलं पण्डितानाम्।
जघनमरुणरत्नग्रन्थिकाञ्चीकलापं
कुवलयनयनानां को विहातुं समर्थः ॥29॥

उन्मत्त प्रेमसंरम्भात आरभन्ते यदङ्गनाः।
तत्र प्रत्यूहमाधातुं ब्रह्मापि खलु कातरः ॥30॥

विश्वामित्रपराशरप्रभृतयो वाताम्बुपर्णाशना-
स्तेऽपि स्त्रीमुखपङ्कजं सुललितं दृष्ट्वैव मोहं गताः।
शाल्यन्नं सघृतं पयोदधियुतं भुञ्जन्ति ये मानवा-
स्तेषामिन्द्रियनिग्रहो यदि भवेद्विन्ध्यस्तरेत्सागरम् ॥31॥

God guard us from these doe-eyed women's eyes
Which can at times disturb even the wise.
The tittle lamp of wisdom strenuously lit
One amorous glance from them can like an arrow hit.

The bookful blockheads preaching self-restraint
Do not consider what's really at stake.
Love's play on passionate breasts and thighs once known,
Such amorous raptures who can ever forsake?

O, once a woman is on Love intent
And sets about it with full armament,
Not even Brahma...lord-creator can
To her victorious course admit impediment.

Sages like Vishwamitra and Parashar-
Who can subsist on leaves and air and water,
Could not resist the nymphs who tempted them.
Of gluttons like us what will then become?

सुधाशुभ्रं धाम स्फुरदमलरश्मिः शशधरः
प्रियावक्त्राम्भोजं मलयजरजश्चातिसुरभिः।
स्रजो हृद्यामोदास्तदिदमखिलं रागिणि जने
करोत्यन्तः क्षोभं न तु विषयसंसर्गविमुखे ॥32॥

तरुणीवैषा दीपितकामा विकसितजातिः पुण्यसुगन्धिः
उन्नतपीनपयोधरभारा प्रावट् तनुते कस्य न हर्षम् ॥33॥

वियदुपचितमेघं भूमयः कन्दलिन्यो
नवकुटजकदम्बामोदिनी गन्धवाहाः।
शिखिकुलकलकेकारावरम्या वनान्ताः
सुखिनमसुखिनं वा सर्वमुत्कण्ठयन्ति ॥34॥

उपरि घनं घनपटलं तिर्यग्गिरयोऽपि नर्तितमयूराः।
क्षितिरपि कन्दलधवला दृष्टिं पथिकः क्व यापयतु ॥35॥

A whitewashed house, full moon, a beloved face,
Garlands of fragrant flowers, Sandal pure
All things can vex a prisoner of five senses
But not the sage, who has o'ercome their lure.

How can the rainy season fail to charm
Who has so much in common with young girls!
Aroused desire, full-blown fragrant blossoms,
Clouds swelling like their ripening breasts and curls.

The sky o'ercast with swelling, curling cloud
Earth sprouting everywhere and breezes proud
Bearing sweet incense; peacocks shouting mad
Fill all with longing, whether glad or sad.

Above, the canopy of clouds; below the peacock's prancing;
The hills around seem joining hands as if to them advancing.
The earth too clad in green is in a mood to celebrate
Poor traveller, far from home is both dejected and elate.

असूची संसारे तमसि नभसि प्रौढजलद
ध्वनिप्राये तस्मिन्पतति दृषदां नीरनिचये।
इदं सौदामिन्या कनककमनीय विलसितं
मुदं च ग्लानिं प्रथयति पथिष्वेव सुदृशाम् ॥36॥

अर्ध नीत्वा निशायाः सरभससुरतायासखिन्नश्लथाङ्गः
प्रोद्भूतासह्यतृष्णो मधुमदनिरतो हर्म्यपृष्ठे विविक्ते।
संभोगक्लान्तकान्ताशिथिलभुजलतावर्जितं कर्करीतो
ज्योत्स्नाभिन्नाच्छधारं पिबति न सलिलं शारदं मन्दभाग्यः ॥37॥

It's pitch dark—Earth and Sky in silence waiting
For rain to join them—'absence is the longing
For presence'—that is what the thunder said.
The earlier lightning message this confirming.

Midnight—a love-intoxicated couple
Have just emerged from their bewilderment.
A moonlight thread of water poured by beloved hands
To slake his thirst. How lucky to have lived through such enchantment!

VAIRAGYA ŚATAKA
वैराग्य शतक

चूडोत्तंसितचन्द्रचारुकलिकाचञ्चच्छिखाभास्वरो
लीलादग्धविलोलकामशलभः श्रेयोदशाग्रे स्फुरन्।
अन्तः स्फूर्जदपारमोहतिमिरप्राग्भाग्मुच्चाटयं–
श्वेतःसद्मनि योगिनां विजयते ज्ञानप्रदीपो हरः ॥1॥

यावत्स्वस्थमिदं कलेवरगृहं यावच्च दूरे जरा
यावच्चेन्द्रियशक्तिप्रतिहता यावत्क्षयो नायुषः।
आत्मश्रेयसि तावदेव विदुषा कार्यः प्रयत्नो महान्
प्रोद्दीप्ते भवने च कूपखननं प्रत्युद्यमः कीदृशः ॥2॥

बोद्धारो मत्सरग्रस्ताः प्रभवः स्मयदूषिताः।
अबोधोपहताश्चान्ये जीर्णमंङ्गे सुभाषितम् ॥3॥

Blessings I invoke of Śiva, Lord of this wide universe:
Dwelling in the heart of Yogis who doth spark-like thence disperse
Every atom of ignorance spread by the world's contagion foul,
Blessing with supreme ecstasy their ancient aspiring soul.

While blessed breathings wait upon your frame
And deadening wintertime of life is far;
While limbs are not rendered diseased and lame
The well of life undried; and hale you are;
Your foremost duty is, as sages tell
To strive to know yourself, the lustre pure.
It's but a fool who starts to dig a well
When fast the hungry flames his house devour.

Small wonder if the fruits of learning be
Condemned fore'er to mediocrity;
For the scholars are all torn by jealousy
And others feed just on their vanity.

न संसारोत्पन्नं चरितमनुपश्यामि कुशलं
विपाकः पुण्यानां जनयति भयं मे विमृशतः।
महद्भिः पुण्यौघैश्चिरपरिगृहीताश्च विषया
महान्तो जायन्ते व्यसनमिव दातुं विषयिणाम् ॥4॥

उत्खातं निधिशङ्कया क्षितितलं ध्माता गिरेर्धातवो
निस्तीर्णः सरितां पतिनृपतयो यत्नेन सन्तोषिताः।
मन्त्राराधनतत्परेण मनसा नीताः श्मशाने निशाः
प्राप्तः काणवराटकोऽपि न मया तृष्णेऽधुना मुञ्च माम् ॥5॥

भ्रान्तं देशमनेकदुर्गविषमं प्राप्तं न किञ्चित्फलं
त्यक्त्वा जाति कुलाभिमानमुचितं सेवा कृता निष्फला।
भुक्तं मानविवर्जितं परगृहे साशङ्कया काकवत्
तृष्णे दुर्मतिपापकर्मनिरते नाऽद्यापि सन्तुष्यसि ॥6॥

कृतश्चित्तस्तम्भः प्रहसित धियामञ्जलिरपि
त्वमाशे मोघाशे किमपरमतो नर्तयसि माम ॥7॥

This earth holds not a single creature blest;
Thoughts of hereafter cause a great unrest.
The righteous might his fruits in heaven reap;
His sufferings here still keep my heart depress't.

0 devilish Greed! Thou foe of man accurst!
Who dost propel him on to actions worst
Black magic, flattery, shameful self betrayal
Still must thou rise and he be sin-immersed.

Hast thou not suffered in thy quest of gold
Pain, hazards and humiliations untold?
While thy poor neighbour prized his honour most,
Thy honour for a trinket hath been sold.

Foul Greed, with her strings puppet-like me sway'd
And to such meanness did my 'self' degrade,
That mine was life of deadliest servitude
By every human grace left desolate.

व्यापारे बहुकार्य भारगुरुभिः कालो न विज्ञायते।
दृष्ट्वा जन्मजराविपत्तिमरणं त्रासश्च नोत्पद्यते
पीत्वा मोहमयीं प्रमादमदिरामुन्मत्त भूतं जगत् ॥8॥

दीना दीनमुखैः सदैव शिशुकैराकृष्ट जीर्णाम्बरा
क्रोशद्भिःक्षुधितैर्नरैर्न विधुरा दृश्येत चेद् गेहिनी।
याञ्चाभङ्गभयेन गद्गदलसत्त्रुट्यद्विलीनाक्षरं
को देहीति वदेत्स्वदग्धजठरस्यार्थे मनस्वी जनः ॥9॥

निवृत्ता भोगेच्छा पुरुषबहुमानो विगलितः
समानाः स्वर्याताः सपदि सुहृदो जीवित समाः।
शनैर्यष्ट्योत्थानं घनतिमिररुद्धे च नयने
अहो धृष्टः कायस्तदपि मरणापाय चकितः ॥10॥

न ध्यातं पदमीश्वरस्य विधिवत्संसारविच्छित्तये
स्वर्गद्वारकपाटपाटनपटुर्धर्मोऽपि नोपार्जितः।
नारीपीनपयोधरोरुयुगलं स्वप्नेऽपि नालिङ्गितं
मातुः केवलमेव यौवनवनच्छेदे कुठारा वयम् ॥11॥

Drunk with Delusion's ever-tempting wine
We mortals fail to see the spark divine.
Caught in the vicious whirl of nights and days
Our soul never stops to think of its decline.

Why staggerest thou to see that strong-will'd man
With folded hands beseech the rich villain?
He could not bear the sight of his loved ones;
Starvation facing, who can whole remain?

Spent are all passions and the fret for fame;
Dim grows the sight; fast fails the tottering frame;
Old friends beloved have vanished one by one,
Oh me! Still Death remains a horrid name.

Pang seizes me when I reflect how vain
And void a tenor did my life retain:
Hesitant for e'er the joys of life to taste
Nor given to God, I ne'er could bliss attain.

भोगा न भुक्ता वयमेव भुक्तास्तपो न तप्तं वयमेव तप्ताः।
कालो न यातो वयमेव यातास्तृष्णा न जीर्णा वयमेव जीर्णाः ॥12॥

बलिभिर्मुखमाक्रान्तं पलितैरंकितं शिरः।
गात्राणि शिथिलायन्ते तृष्णैका तरुणायते ॥13॥

क्षान्तं न क्षमया गृहोचितसुखं त्यक्तं न संतोषतः
सोढा दुःसहशीतवाततपनाः क्लेशान्न तप्तं तपः।
ध्यातं वित्तमहर्निशं नियमितप्राणैर्न शंभोः पदं
तत्तत्कर्म कृतं यदेव मुनिभिस्तैस्तैः फलैर्वञ्चितम् ॥14॥

भिक्षाशनं तदपि नीरसमेकवारं
शय्या च भूः परिजनो निजदेहमात्रम्।
वस्त्रं च जीर्णशतखण्डमयीचकन्था
हा हा तथापि विषया न परित्यजन्ति ॥15॥

The spring of Life knows drying not a bit
But we are too worn-out to taste of it.
Time hath kill'd us; not we it, as we thought
Life dwindles; but Desire!—Not a whit.

My face with wrinkles is invaded fast;
Before my mirrored 'gray' I stand aghast.
Old age hath of its strength my body robbed;
Young still Desire keeps as in the past.

What, if restraint of self be forced on you
By circumstance, composure would ensue
Only, when you at your own sweet will shunned
Temptations and attained detachment true.

Earth is my bed and quilt of scrappings waste;
My food receipt in alms devoid of taste;
Friendless I roam; but still, Oh, woe is me:
Still pursue me the hounds of thoughts unchaste.

फलमलमशनाय स्वादु पानाय तोयं
शयनमवनिपृष्ठं वल्कलं वाससो च
नवधनमधुपानभ्रान्त सर्वेन्द्रियाणा-
मविनयमनुमन्तुं नोत्सहे दुर्जनानाम् ॥16॥

अजानन्माहात्म्यं पततु शलभो दीपदहने
स मीनोऽप्यज्ञानाद् वडिशयुतमश्नातु पिशितम्।
विजानन्तोऽप्येतद् वयमिह विपज्जालजटिलात्
न मुञ्चामः कामानहह! गहनो मोहमहिमा ॥17॥

विपुलहृदयैर्धन्यैः कैश्चिज्जगज्जनितं पुरा
विधृतमपरैर्दत्तं चान्यैर्विजित्य तृणं यथा
इह हि भुवनान्यन्ये धीराश्चतुर्दश भुञ्जते
कतिपय पुरस्वाम्ये पुंसां क एष मदज्वरः ॥18॥

त्वं राजा वयमप्युपासित गुरु प्रज्ञाभिमानोन्नताः
ख्यातस्त्वं विभवैर्यशांसि कवयो दिक्षु प्रतन्वन्ति नः।
इत्थमानद नातिदूरमुभयोरप्यावयोरन्तरं
यद्यस्मासु पराङ्मुखोऽसि वयमप्येकान्ततो निःस्पृहाः ॥19॥

How can the pride of wealth dare slight the saint
Who lives in solitude free from all taint.
Wild fruits of forest are his sustenance;
Bare earth his bed; bark of the trees garment.

The moth doth burn itself in ignorance.
Scarce can the fish their Death in the bait sense.
Though we are neither, still into pitfalls oft
We are betray'd, for all our vigilance.

Conceited kings puffed up with gains so scant!
Hast thou e'er thought or heard of heroes old
Who first the treasures of this wide earth scann'd
Before whose will rough Nature turned pliant?

If you're a king, we have our grandeur too.
The radiance of our minds doth far outdo
That of thy gold; thy fame is put to shame
Before our name that spreads the wide world through.

मृत्पिण्डो जलरेखया वलयितः सर्वोऽप्ययं नन्वणु-
रङ्गीकृत्य स एव संयुगशतै राज्ञां गणैर्भुज्यते।
तद्दद्युर्ददतेऽथ वा न किमपि क्षुद्रा दरिद्रा भृशं
धिक्धिक्तान्पुरुषाधमान्धनकणं वाञ्छन्ति तेभ्योऽपि ये ॥20॥

पुरा विद्वत्तासीदुपशमवतां क्लेशहतये
गता कालेनासौ विषयसुखसिद्ध्यै विषयिणाम्।
इदानीं तु प्रेक्ष्य क्षितितलभुजः शास्त्रविमुखा-
नहो कष्टं साऽपि प्रतिदिनमधोऽधः प्रविशति ॥21॥

स जातः कोप्यासीन्मदनरिपुणा मूर्ध्नि धवलं
कपालं यस्योच्चैर्विनिहितमलङ्कारविषये।
नृभिः प्राणत्राणप्रवणमतिभिः कैश्चिदधुना
नमद्भिः कः पुंसामयमतुलदर्पज्वरभरः ॥22॥

अर्थानामाशिषे त्वं वयमपि च गिरामीशमहे यावदर्थं
शूरस्त्वं वादिदर्पज्वरशमनविधावक्षयं पाटवं नः।
सेवन्ते त्वां धनाढ्या मतिमलहतये मामपि श्रोतुकामा
मय्यप्यास्था न चेत्तत्वयि मम सुतराम् एष राजन्गतोऽस्मि ॥23॥

A lump of clay by water girdled round—
This earth is daily swept by battle-sound.
Vain are those kings that for its fragments strive;
Cursed be those wretches whom their tales astound.

An end in itself, knowledge still could be
used in days ancient men from pain to free.
From closets then to courts t'was levell'd down.
Kings too indifferent—sinks it rapidly.

Hast thou not of that king among men heard—
Whose spirit's might Lord Śiva himself admired,
That thou vain creature, art with pride so drunk
With one obsequious bow or flatt'ring word?

Give not thyself such airs; you cannot hold
Thy own before us who have wealth untold—
That grows with spending and such splendour hath
As shames thy valour and bedims thy gold.

अतिक्रान्तः कालो लटभललना भोगसुभगो
भ्रमन्तः श्रान्ताःस्मः सुचिरमिह संसारसरणौ।
इदानीं स्वः सिन्धोस्तटभुवि समाक्रन्दनगिरः
सुतारैः फूत्कारैः शिव शिव शिवेति प्रतनुमः ॥24॥

परेषां चेतांसि प्रतिदिवसमाराध्य बहुधा
प्रसादं किं नेतुं विशसि हृदयं क्लेशकलितम्।
प्रसन्ने त्वय्यन्तः स्वयमुदितचिन्तामणिगुणे
विमुक्तः संकल्पः किमभिलषितं पुष्यति न ते ॥25॥

भोगे रोगभयं कुले च्युतिभयं वित्ते नृपालाद्भयम्
मौने दैन्यभयं बले रिपुभयं रूपे जराया भयम्।
शास्त्रे वादभयं गुणे खलभयं काये कृतान्ताद्भयं
सर्वं वस्तु भयान्वितं भुवि नृणां वैराग्यमेवाभयम् ॥26॥

अमीषां प्राणानां तुलितबिसनीपत्रपयसां
कृते किम् अस्माभिः विगलितविवेकैः व्यवसितम्।
यदाढ्यानामग्रे द्रविणमदनिःशंकमनसां
कृतं वीतव्रीडैर्निजगुणकथापातकमपि ॥27॥

Too old, too old am I a wench to taste.
And endless wanderings drag my frame to waste.
To the bank of Ganges must I hence retire
And chant Lord Śiva's name immersed to waist.

Dost thou think thou shalt perfect bliss attain
By flatte'ring others? Cease then from this pain.
And be thy own upholder, saint and guide.
Win freedom for thy mind; thyself remain.

The fear of illness mars all enjoyment;
Power dreads foes; Merit the malignant.
Our life is fraught with fear; Deliverance is
Wrought in the renunciation of the saint.

Short-lived e'en as the water-drops on blade,
Our life away recklessly let we fade
In barrenness; and for some wretched crumbs
Before the rich, prostrate ourselves laid.

उद्रिक्तः स च राजपुत्र निवहस्ते वन्दिनस्ताः कथाः
सर्वं यस्य वशादगात्स्मृतिपथं कालाय तस्मै तमः ॥28॥

वयं येभ्यो जाताश्चिरपरिगता एव खलु ते
समं यैः संवृद्धाः स्मृतिविषयतां तेऽपि गमिताः ।
इदानीमेते स्म प्रतिदिवसमासन्नपतनात्–
गतास्तुल्यावस्थां सिकतिलनदीतीरतरुभिः ॥29॥

यत्रानेकः क्वचिदपि गृहे तत्र तिष्ठत्यथैको
यत्राप्येकस्तदनु बहवस्तत्र चान्ते न चैकः ।
इत्थं चेमौ रजनिदिवसौ दोलयन्द्धाविवाक्षौ
कालः काल्या सह बहुकलः क्रीडति प्राणिशारैः ॥30॥

तपस्यन्तः सन्तः किमधिनिवसामः सुरनदीं
गुणोदारान्दारानुत परिचरामः सविनयम् ।
पिबामः शास्त्रौघात् द्रुतविविध काव्यामृतरसात्
न विद्मः किं कुर्मः कतिपय निमेषायुषि जने ॥31॥

Where is the glory, in these ruins which grew
But once;—the king with the gorgeous retinue?
Time swallowed all, reducing to a name
The many-splendoured state and statesmen too.

The authors of this life did long outsoar
This world, and dead too are our friends of yore.
And we're like sand-bank trees;...One giant wave
And then our place will know us not—no more.

The house where one lived, is with many fill'd;
Where once lived many, Death his spite hath spill'd,
Who joined with Time with us as pieces plays
On this vast Board the ancient game as willed.

My mortal moments!—Know not I what use
Shall they be put to; tempting is the noose.
But greater far the rapture of th'recluse.
Or leave it all; and let me serve the muse.

गंगातीरे हिमगिरिशिलाबद्धपद्मासनस्य
ब्रह्मध्यानाभ्यसनविधिना योगनिद्रां गतस्य।
किं तैर्भाव्यं मम सुदिवसैर्यत्र ते निर्विशंकाः
संप्राप्स्यन्ते जरठहरिणाः शृंङ्गकंडूविनोदम् ॥32॥

स्फुरत्स्फारज्योत्स्नाधवलिततले क्वापि पुलिने
सुखासीनाः शान्तध्वनिषु रजनीषु द्युसरितः।
भवाभोगोद्विग्नाः शिवशिवशिवेत्यार्तवचसा
कदा स्यामाऽऽनन्दोद्गतबहुलवाष्पप्लुतदृशा ॥33॥

महादेवो देवः सरिदपि च सैषा सुरसरिद्-
गुहा एवागारं वसनमपि ता एव हरितः।
सुहृद्वा कालोऽयं व्रतमिदमदैन्यं व्रतमिति
कियद्वा वक्ष्यामो वटविटप एवास्तु दयिता ॥34॥

आशा नाम नदी मनोरथजला तृष्णा तरङ्गाकुला
रागग्राहवती वितर्कविहगा धैर्यद्रुमध्वंसिनी।
मोहावर्तसुदुस्तराऽतिगहना प्रोत्तुङ्गचिन्तातटी
तस्याः पारगता विशुद्धमनसो नन्दन्ति योगीश्वराः ॥35॥

O God! should it be ever mine to see
The day when perfect, sweet serenity
Blessing my spirit, my corporeal frame
To pain and pleasure will indifferent be?

O for the days when sitting on the grand
And moon-blanched bank of holy Ganga's sand
My eyes overflowing with the tears of love
Lord Śiva's name enraptured shall I chant?

My Lord is Śiva and home this lonely cave.
My garment air; companion Ganga's wave;
The arms of Bunyan like a faithful wife
Spread o'er my head; what more have I to crave?

Hope is a stream that waves of longings sweep
And where allurements crocodile-like creep.
The tree of peace its frantic surge uproots.
Few, few can 'scape its whirlpools dark and deep.

गात्रेगिरा च विकलश्चटुमीश्वराणां
कुर्वन्नयं प्रहसनस्य नटः कृतोऽसि
तं त्वा पुनः पलितवर्ण कभाजमेनं
नाट्येन केन नटयिष्यति दीर्घमायुः ॥36॥

वितीर्णे सर्वस्वे तरुणकरुणापूर्णहृदयाः
स्मरन्तः संसारे विगुणपरिणामावधिगतीः ।
वयं पुण्यारण्ये परिणतशरच्चन्द्रकिरणैः
स्त्रियामां नेष्यामो हरचरणचित्तैकशरणाः ॥37॥

वयमिह परितुष्टा वल्कलैस्त्वं च लक्ष्म्या
सम इह परितोषो निर्विशेषावशेषः ।
स तु भवति दरिद्रो यस्य तृष्णा विशाला
मनसि च परितुष्टे कोऽर्थवान् को दरिद्रः ॥38॥

यदेतत्स्वच्छन्दं विहरणमकार्पण्यमशनं
सहायैः संवासः श्रुतमुपशमैकव्रतफलम् ।
मनो मन्दस्पन्दं बहिरपि चिरस्यापि विमृश-
न्न जाने कस्यैषा परिणतिरुदारस्य तपसः ॥39॥

Reclining on my cavern's lone rock-bed
From trance awaken'd, memories fill my head,
Of days in soul-debasing flattery spent
Or in cheap pleasures, and I shrink in dread.

Assured in mind that all is vanity,
I gave the poor my all in charity.
Now in my moon-lit forest hermitage
I pass my days in perfect liberty.

Clad we're in barks; and thou in silk and gold.
But still our content sweeter is; behold
The poorest wretch is he who craves all life.
Wealth and want are the same to the tranquil-souled.

What righteous deed I know not could procure
An air-like freedom and a living pure;
Knowledge of scriptures, and a quiet mind
That tasteth things yet conquers every lure.

पाणिः पात्रं पवित्रं भ्रमणपरिगतं भैक्षमक्षय्यमन्नं
विस्तीर्णं वस्त्रमाशासुदशकममलं तल्पमस्वल्पमुर्वी।
येषां निःसंगतांगीकरणपरिणतिः स्वात्मसन्तोषिणस्ते
धन्याः संन्यस्तदैन्यव्यतिकरनिकराः कर्म निर्मूलयन्ति ॥40॥

भोगा मेघवितानमध्यविलसत् सौदामिनी चञ्चला
आयुः वायु विघटिताभ्र पटलीनाम्बुद्भङ्गरम्।
लीला यौवनलालसा तनुभृतामित्याकलय्य द्रुतं
योगे धैर्यसमाधिसिद्धिसुलभे बुद्धिं विधद्ध्वं बुधाः ॥41॥

चाण्डालः किमयं द्विजातिरथवा शूद्रोऽथ किं तापसः
किवा तत्त्वनिवेशपेशलमतिः योगीश्वरः कोऽपि किम्।
इत्युत्पन्नविकल्पजल्पमुखरैः सम्भाष्यमाणा जनैर्न
क्रुद्धाः पथि नैव तुष्टमनसो यान्ति स्वयं योगिनः ॥42॥

एतस्माद्विरमेन्द्रियार्थ गहनादायासकादाश्रय
श्रेयोमार्गमशेष दुःखशमनव्यापारदक्षं क्षणात्।
शान्तं भावमुपैहि संत्यज निजां कल्लोललोलां गतिं
मा भूयो भज भंगुरां भवरतिं चेतः प्रसीदाधुना ॥43॥

Blest are the saints who from all passions free
Possess their souls and live in ecstasy—
With boundless space as garment and a bowl
Of rice as food and woods as company.

As lightning's fickle dance is to the clouds,
So are our joys to us; the youth that blooms
Amid a world of loveliest dreams knows not
How large the shadow of death on him looms.

The yogi walked; they started and beheld;
All sorts of idle sneers on him hurled;
All this he heard and smiled and heeded not.
He—master of himself and all this world.

Too long, too long in this bewildering maze
Of world thou hast been wand'ring; Change thy ways.
Oh, Desist from this wayward wavelike course
And teach thyself the quiet of the sage.

सखे धन्याः केचित्त्रुटितभवबन्धव्यतिकरा
वनान्ते चित्तान्तर्विषमविषयाशीविषगताः।
शरच्चन्द्रज्योत्स्नाधवलगगनाभोगसुभगां
नयन्ते ये रात्रिं सुकृतचयचित्तैकशरणाः ॥44॥

आयुः कल्लोललोलं कतिपयदिवसस्थायिनी यौवनश्री-
अर्थाः संकल्पकल्पा घनसमयतड़िद्विभ्रमा भोगपूराः।
कण्ठाश्लेषोपगूढ़ः तदपि च न चिरं यत्प्रियाभिः प्रणीतं
ब्रह्मण्यासक्तचित्ता भवत भवभयाम्भोधिपारं तरीतुम् ॥45॥

गङ्गातरङ्गकणशीकरशीतलानि
विद्याधराध्युषितचारुशिलातलानि।
स्थानानि किं हिमवतः प्रलयं गतानि
यत्सावमानपरपिण्डरता मनुष्याः ॥46॥

यदा मेरुः श्रीमान्निपतति युगान्ताग्निनिहतः
समुद्राः शुष्यन्ति प्रचुरमकरग्राहनिलयाः।
धरा गच्छत्यन्तं धरणिधरपादैरपि धृता
शरीरे का वार्त्ता करिकरभकर्णाग्रचपले ॥47॥

Once, having freed myself from this foul mire
To jungle solitudes I now retire...
Where wintry winds of all this wanton world
Dare threaten not my spirit's sacred fire.

The strongest wave doth soon itself exhaust;
And so too fire, to nothingess is lost;
The lightning having danced a little while;
And so our life like bubbles soon will burst.

The forests still their fruits in plenty yield.
And barks could thee from rains and tempests shield.
Why dost thou for some wretched crumbs beseech
those who themselves before others have kneel'd?

The fancy-staggering works of earth and sea
Are from Annihilation's gaze not free.
The very earth is vexed with tremors wild
Doth thought of it not shame thy vanity?

पातालमाविशसि यासि नभो विलंघ्य
दिग्मण्डलं भ्रमसि मानसचापलेन।
भ्रान्त्यापि जातु विमलं कथमात्मनीतं
तद्ब्रह्म न स्मरसि निर्वृतिमेषि येन ॥48॥

रात्रिः सैव पुनः स एव दिवसो मत्वा बुधा जन्तवो
धावन्त्युद्यमिनस्तथैव निभृतप्रारब्धतत्तत्क्रियाः।
व्यापारैः पुनरुक्तभुक्तविषयैरेवंविधेनामुना
संसारेण कदर्थिता कथमहो मोहान्न लज्जामहे ॥49॥

मही रम्या शय्या विपुलमुपधानं भुजलता
वितानं चाकाशं व्यजनमनुकूलोऽयमनिलः।
स्फुरद्दीपचन्द्रो विरतिवनितासङ्गमुदितः
सुखं शान्तः शेते मुनिरतनुभूतिर्नृप इव ॥50॥

रम्याश्चन्द्रमरीचयस्तृणवती रम्या वनस्थली
रम्यः साधुसमागमः शमसुखं काव्येषु रम्याः कथाः।
कोपोपाहितवाष्पबिन्दुतरलं रम्यं प्रियाया मुखं
सर्वरम्यमनित्यतामुपगते चित्ते न किंचित्पुनः ॥51॥

The skies may all their secrets yield to thee;
To thee may show their riches earth and sea.
All this, alas, poor soul! availeth nought:
Know thyself and bliss perfect thine shall be.

Day dawns, and soon night's wheels will rattle fast;
Our present but repeats the weary Past;
Yet to the scheme of things so vain and stale
We cling and think our days will ever last.

Pillow'd upon his arm and flatter'd by
Sweet gales beneath the canopy of sky:
With resignation's spouse his heart to bless
The sage reclines king-like in majesty.

Sweet are the meadows blanch'd by rays serene
Of moon; and sweeter still the pleasures keen
Of love and verse. What charm they have for me
Who know how transient have all such things been.

मातर्मेदिनि तात मारुत सखे तेजः सुबन्धो जल
भ्रातर्व्योम निबद्ध एव भवतामेष प्रणामाञ्जलिः
युष्मत्सङ्गवशोपजात सुकृतोद्रेक स्फुरन्निर्मल-
ज्ञानमपास्तसमस्त मोहमहिमा लीये परब्रह्मणि ॥52॥

भोगा भंगुरवृत्तयो बहुविधास्तैरेव चायं भव-
स्तत्कस्येव कृते परिभ्रमतरे लोकाः कृतं चेष्टितैः।
आशापाशशतोपशान्तिविशदं चेतः समाधीयतां
कामोच्छित्तिहरे स्वधामनि यदि श्रद्धेयमस्मद्वचः ॥53॥

गात्रं संकुचितं गतिर्विगलिता भ्रष्टा च दन्तावलि
दृष्टिर्नश्यति वर्धते बधिरता वक्त्रं च लालायते।
वाक्यं नाद्रियते च बान्धवजनो भार्या न शुश्रूषते
हा कष्टं पुरुषस्य जीर्णवयसः पुत्रोऽप्यमित्रायते ॥54॥

बाले लीलामुकुलितमयी मन्थरा दृष्टिपाताः
किं क्षिप्यन्ते विरम विरम व्यर्थ एष श्रमस्ते।
सम्प्रत्यन्ये वयमुपरतं बाल्यमास्था वनान्ते
क्षीणो मोहस्तृणमिव जगज्जालमालोकयामः ॥55॥

O mother Earth! Friend sky and Father Air!
I bow to thee with folded hands in prayer,
Thy contact all my guilt hath washed away—
Bathing my mind in radiance...every layer.

Axe-like Desire killed our modesty;
And made us lick the boots of Vanity;
Woe for the time and we shall now be free;
And breathe the air of wholesome poverty.

Old man! remembrance of the good old days
Will only make 'now' worse; the son that pays
No heed to thee; the wife turned indifferent.
Why staggerest thou?...These are but the world's ways.

Don't cast inviting glances at me, girl!
No longer am I by such signals stirred.
I did sow wild oats once; but have changed since.
I have cut off all snares of this world.

विरमत बुधा योषित्सङ्गात् सुखात् क्षणभंगुरात्
कुरुत करुणामैत्रीप्रज्ञावधूजन सङ्गमम्।
न खलु नरके हाराक्रान्तं धनस्तनमण्डलं
शरणमथवा श्रोणीबिम्बं रणन्मणिमेखलम् ॥56॥

क्षणं बालो भूत्वा क्षणमपि युवा कामरसिकः
क्षणं वित्तैर्हीनः क्षणमपि च सम्पूर्णविभवः।
जराजीर्णैरङ्गैर्नट इव वलीमण्डिततनु-
र्नरः संसारान्ते विशति यमधानी जवनिकाम् ॥57॥

The joy companionship of women brings
End in despair and disillusionment.
Self-knowledge is the only certain good
Leading to calm of mind, all passion spent.

Back, whence you came, your hour O man, is spent
Upon this stage where first a babe you went;
And then as youth, your feverish part enacted,
you played the wrinkled Age; and now...'The End'.

❑❑❑